SCARY STORIES
TO TELL
IN THE DARK

ALSO BY
ALVIN SCHWARTZ

More Scary Stories to Tell in the Dark

Scary Stories 3
More Tales to Chill Your Bones

I Can Read Books™
(for younger readers)

All of Our Noses Are Here
and Other Noodle Tales

Ghosts!
Ghostly Tales from Folklore

I Saw You in the Bathtub
and Other Folk Rhymes

In a Dark, Dark Room
and Other Scary Stories

There Is a Carrot in My Ear
and Other Noodle Tales

SCARY STORIES
TO TELL
IN THE DARK

COLLECTED FROM FOLKLORE
AND RETOLD BY
ALVIN SCHWARTZ

ILLUSTRATED BY
BRETT HELQUIST

HARPER
An Imprint of HarperCollinsPublishers

Library of Congress catalog card number: 2009934072
ISBN 978-0-06-083519-4 (trade bdg.)
ISBN 978-0-06-083520-0 (pbk.)

Typography by Torborg Davern
17 PC/LSCH 11
❖
Reillustrated edition, 2010

"The Thing" is adapted from an untitled story in *Bluenose Ghosts* by Helen Creighton with permission of McGraw-Hill Ryerson Ltd., Toronto. Copyright 1957 by The Ryerson Press.

"The Haunted House" is adapted from a story of that title in *American Folk Tales and Songs* by Richard Chase with permission of Dover Publications. Copyright 1956 by Richard Chase, 1971 by Dover Publications.

"Aaron Kelly's Bones" is adapted from "Daid Aaron II" in *Doctor to the Dead* by John Bennett with permission of Russell & Volkening, Inc., as agents for the author. Copyright 1943, 1971 by Mr. Bennett.

"Me Tie Dough-ty Walker!" is adapted from the tale "The Rash Dog and the Bloody Head," which appeared in the *Hoosier Folklore Bulletin*, vol. 1, 1942. Used by permission of Dr. Herbert Halpert, collector of the tale.

"Alligators" is adapted from "The Alligator Story" in *Sticks in the Knapsack and Other Ozark Folk Tales* by Vance Randolph with permission of the Columbia University Press. Copyright 1958 by the Columbia University Press.

"The White Wolf" is adapted from a story of that title in *The Telltale Lilac Bush and Other West Virginia Ghost Tales* by Ruth Ann Musick with permission of the University of Kentucky Press. Copyright 1965 by the University of Kentucky Press.

"A New Horse" is adapted from the tale "Bridling the Witch" in *Up Cutshin and Down Greasy: The Couches' Tales and Songs* (reprinted as *Sang Branch Settlers: Folksongs and Tales of an Eastern Kentucky Family*) by Leonard W. Roberts with permission of Dr. Roberts. Copyright 1980 by Leonard W. Roberts.

The musical notation on page 20 and page 39 was transcribed and illustrated by Melvin Wildberger.

CONTENTS

To Dinah

—A. S.

SCARY STORIES
TO TELL
IN THE DARK

STRANGE AND
SCARY THINGS

Pioneers used to entertain themselves by telling scary stories. At night they might gather in somebody's cabin, or around a fire, and see who could scare the others the most.

Some girls and boys in my town do the same thing today. They get together at somebody's house, and they turn out the lights and eat popcorn, and scare one another half to death.

Telling scary stories is something people have done for thousands of years, for most of us *like* being scared in that way. Since there isn't any danger, we think it is fun.

There are a great many scary stories to tell. There are ghost stories. There are tales of witches, devils, bogeymen, zombies, and vampires. There are tales of monstrous creatures and of other dangers. There even are stories that make us laugh at all this scariness.

Some of these tales are very old, and they are told

around the world. And most have the same origins. They are based on things that people saw or heard or experienced—or thought they did.

Many years ago a young prince became famous for a scary story he started to tell, but did not finish. His name was Mamillius, and he probably was nine or ten years old. William Shakespeare told about him in *The Winter's Tale*.

It was on a dark winter's day that his mother, the queen, asked him for a story.

"A sad tale's best for winter," he said. "I have one of sprites and goblins."

"Do your best to frighten me with your sprites," she said. "You're powerful at it."

"I shall tell it softly," he said. "Yond crickets shall not hear it."

And he began, "There was a man dwelt by a churchyard." But that was as far as he got. For at that moment the king came in and arrested the queen and took her away. And soon after that, Mamillius died. No one knows how he would have finished his story. If you started as he did, what would you tell?

Most scary stories are, of course, meant to be told. They are more scary that way. But *how* you tell them is important.

As Mamillius knew, the best way is to speak

softly, so that your listeners lean forward to catch your words, and to speak slowly, so that your voice sounds scary.

And the best time to tell these stories is at night. In the dark and the gloom, it is easy for someone listening to imagine all sorts of strange and scary things.

Princeton, New Jersey   ALVIN SCHWARTZ

"AAAAAAAAAAAH!"

*This chapter is filled with "jump stories"
you can use to make your friends
JUMP with fright.*

THE BIG TOE

A boy was digging at the edge of the garden when he saw a big toe. He tried to pick it up, but it was stuck to something. So he gave it a good hard jerk, and it came off in his hand. Then he heard something groan and scamper away.

The boy took the toe into the kitchen and showed it to his mother. "It looks nice and plump," she said. "I'll put it in the soup, and we'll have it for supper."

That night his father carved the toe into three pieces, and they each had a piece. Then they did the dishes, and when it got dark they went to bed.

The boy fell asleep almost at once. But in the middle of the night, a sound awakened him. It was something out in the street. It was a voice, and it was calling to him.

"Where is my to-o-o-o-o-e?" it groaned.

When the boy heard that, he got very scared. But he thought, "It doesn't know where I am. It never will find me."

Then he heard the voice once more. Only now it was closer.

"Where is my to-o-o-o-o-e?" it groaned.

The boy pulled the blankets over his head and closed his eyes. "I'll go to sleep," he thought. "When I wake up it will be gone."

But soon he heard the back door open, and again he heard the voice.

"Where is my to-o-o-o-o-e?" it groaned.

Then the boy heard footsteps move through the kitchen into the dining room, into the living room, into the front hall. Then slowly they climbed the stairs.

Closer and closer they came. Soon they were in the upstairs hall. Now they were outside his door.

"Where is my to-o-o-o-o-e?" the voice groaned.

His door opened. Shaking with fear, he listened as the footsteps slowly moved through the dark toward his bed. Then they stopped.

"Where is my to-o-o-o-o-e?" the voice groaned.

(At this point, pause. Then jump at the person next to you and shout:)

"YOU'VE GOT IT!"

THE BIG TOE also has another ending.

When the boy hears the voice calling for its toe, he finds a strange-looking creature up inside the chimney. The boy is so frightened he can't move. He just stands there and stares at it.

Finally he asks: "W-w-w-what you got such big eyes for?"

And the creature answers: "To look you thro-o-o-ugh and thro-o-o-ugh!"

"W-w-w-what you got such big claws for?"

"To scra-a-a-tch up your gra-a-a-a-ve!"

"W-w-w-what you got such a big mouth for?"

"To swallow you who-o-o-le!"

"W-w-w-what you got such sharp teeth for?"

"TO CHOMP YOUR BONES!"

(As you give the last line, pounce on one of your friends.)

THE WALK

My uncle was walking down a lonely dirt road one day. He came upon a man who also was walking down that road. The man looked at my uncle, and my uncle looked at the man. The man was scared of my uncle, and my uncle was scared of that man.

But they kept on walking, and it began to get dark. The man looked at my uncle, and my uncle looked at the man. The man was *very* scared of my uncle, and my uncle was *very* scared of that man.

But they kept on walking, and they came to a big woods. It was getting darker. And the man looked at my uncle, and my uncle looked at the man. The man was *really* scared of my uncle, and my uncle was *really* scared of that man.

But they kept on walking, and deep down into the woods they went. It was getting darker. And the man looked at my uncle, and my uncle looked at the man. The man was *terrible* scared of my uncle, and my uncle was *terrible* scared of—

(Now SCREAM!)

"WHAT DO YOU COME FOR?"

There was an old woman who lived all by herself, and she was very lonely. Sitting in the kitchen one night, she said, "Oh, I wish I had some company."

No sooner had she spoken than down the chimney tumbled two feet from which the flesh had rotted. The old woman's eyes bulged with terror.

Then two legs dropped to the hearth and attached themselves to the feet.

Then a body tumbled down, then two arms, and a man's head.

As the old woman watched, the parts came together into a great, gangling man. The man danced around and around the room. Faster and faster he went. Then he stopped, and he looked into her eyes.

"What do you come for?" she asked in a small voice that shivered and shook.

"What do I come for?" he said. "I come—for YOU!"

(As you shout the last words, stamp your foot and jump at someone nearby.)

ME TIE DOUGH-TY WALKER!

There was a haunted house where every night a bloody head fell down the chimney. At least that's what people said. So nobody would stay there overnight.

Then a rich man offered two hundred dollars to whoever would do it. And this boy said he would try if he could have his dog with him. So it was all settled.

The very next night the boy went to the house with his dog. To make it more cheerful, he started a fire in the fireplace. Then he sat in front of the fire and waited, and his dog waited with him.

For a while nothing happened. But a little after midnight he heard someone singing softly and sadly off in the woods. The singing sounded something like this:

"ME TIE DOUGH-TY WALKER!"

"It's just somebody singing," the boy told himself, but he was frightened.

Then his dog answered the song! Softly and sadly, it sang:

"LYNCHEE KINCHY COLLY MOLLY DINGO DINGO!"

The boy could not believe his ears. His dog had never uttered a word before. Then a few minutes later, he heard the singing again. Now it was closer and louder, but the words were the same:

"ME TIE DOUGH-TY WALKER!"

This time the boy tried to stop his dog from answering. He was afraid that whoever was singing would hear it and come after them.

But his dog paid no attention, and again it sang:

"LYNCHEE KINCHY COLLY MOLLY DINGO DINGO"

A half hour later the boy heard the singing

again. Now it was in the backyard, and the song was the same:

"ME TIE DOUGH-TY WALKER!"

Again the boy tried to keep his dog quiet. But the dog sang out louder than ever:

"LYNCHEE KINCHY COLLY MOLLY DINGO DINGO!"

Soon the boy heard the singing again. Now it was coming down the chimney:

"ME TIE DOUGH-TY WALKER!"

The dog sang right back:

"LYNCHEE KINCHY COLLY MOLLY DINGO DINGO!"

Suddenly a bloody head fell out of the chimney. It missed the fire and landed right next to the dog. The dog took one look and fell over—dead from fright.

The head turned and stared at the boy. Slowly it opened its mouth, and—

(Turn to one of your friends and scream:)

"AAAAAAAAAAAH!"

A MAN WHO
LIVED IN LEEDS

Some say this rhyme doesn't mean anything. Others
are not so sure.

There was a man who lived in Leeds;
He filled his garden full of seeds.
And when the seeds began to grow,
It was like a garden filled with snow.
But when the snow began to melt,
It was like a ship without a belt.
And when the ship began to sail,
It was like a bird without a tail.
And when the bird began to fly,
It was like an eagle in the sky.
And when the sky began to roar,
It was like a lion at my door.
(Now drop your voice.)
And when the door began to crack,
It was like a penknife in my back.

And when my back began to bleed—
(Turn out any lights.)
I was dead, dead, dead *indeed*!
(Jump at your friends and scream:)
"AAAAAAAAAAAH!"

OLD WOMAN ALL
SKIN AND BONE

There was an old woman all skin and bone
Who lived near the graveyard all alone.
O-o o-o o-o!
She thought she'd go to church one day
To hear the parson preach and pray.
O-o o-o o-o!
And when she came to the church-house stile
She thought she'd stop and rest awhile.

O-o o-o o-o!
When she came up to the door
She thought she'd stop and rest some more.
O-o o-o o-o!
But when she turned and looked around
She saw a corpse upon the ground.
O-o o-o o-o!
From its nose down to its chin
The worms crawled out, and the worms crawled in.
O-o o-o o-o!
The woman to the preacher said,
"Shall I look like that when I am dead?"
O-o o-o o-o!
The preacher to the woman said,
"You'll look like that when you are dead!"
(Now scream:)
"AAAAAAAAAAAH!"

There was an old wo-man all skin and bone Who

lived near the grave-yard all a-lone. O-o o-o o-o!—

HE HEARD FOOTSTEPS COMING UP THE CELLAR STAIRS. . .

There are ghosts in this chapter.
One comes back as a real person.
Another takes revenge on her murderer.
And there are other strange happenings.

THE THING

Ted Martin and Sam Miller were good friends. They spent a lot of time together. On this particular night they were sitting on a fence near the post office talking about one thing and another.

There was a field of turnips across the road. Suddenly they saw something crawl out of the field and stand up. It looked like a man, but in the dark it was hard to tell for sure. Then it was gone.

But soon it appeared again. It walked halfway

across the road, then it turned around and went back into the field.

Then it came out a third time and started toward them. By now Ted and Sam were scared, and they started running. But when they finally stopped, they decided they were being foolish. They weren't sure what had scared them. So they decided to go back and get a better look.

Pretty soon they saw it, for it was coming to meet them. It was wearing black pants, a white shirt, and black suspenders.

Sam said, "I'm going to try to touch it. Then we'll know if it's real."

He walked up to it and peered into its face. It had bright penetrating eyes sunk deep in its head. It looked like a skeleton.

Ted took one look and screamed, and again he and Sam ran, but this time the skeleton followed them. When they got to Ted's house, they stood in the doorway and watched it. It stayed out in the road for a while. Then it disappeared.

A year later Ted got sick and died. Toward the end, Sam sat up with him every night. The night Ted died, Sam said he looked just like the skeleton.

COLD AS CLAY

A farmer had a daughter for whom he cared more than anything on earth. She fell in love with a farmhand named Jim, but the farmer did not think Jim was good enough for his daughter. To keep them apart, he sent her to live with her uncle on the other side of the county.

Soon after she left, Jim got sick, and he wasted away and died. Everyone said he died of a broken heart. The farmer felt so guilty about Jim's death, he could not tell his daughter what had happened. She continued to think about Jim and the life they might have had together.

One night many weeks later there was a knock on her uncle's door. When the girl opened the door, Jim was standing there.

"Your father asked me to get you," he said. "I came on his best horse."

"Is there anything wrong?" she asked.

"I don't know," he said.

She packed a few things, and they left. She rode behind him, clinging to his waist. Soon he complained of a headache. "It aches something terrible," he told her.

She put her hand on his forehead. "Why, you are as cold as clay," she said. "I hope you are not ill," and she wrapped her handkerchief around his head.

They traveled so swiftly that in a few hours they reached the farm. The girl quickly dismounted and knocked on the door. Her father was startled to see her.

"Didn't you send for me?" she asked.

"No, I didn't," he said.

She turned to Jim, but he was gone and so was the horse. They went to the stable to look for them. The horse was there. It was covered with sweat and trembling with fear. But there was no sign of Jim.

Terrified, her father told her the truth about Jim's death. Then quickly he went to see Jim's parents. They decided to open his grave. The corpse was in its coffin. But around its head they found the girl's handkerchief.

THE WHITE WOLF

The timber wolves around French Creek had gotten out of hand. There were so many wolves, the farmers could not stop them from killing their cattle and sheep. So the state put a bounty on them. It would pay a hunter ten dollars for every wolf pelt he turned in.

A butcher in town named Bill Williams thought that was pretty good money. He stopped working as a butcher and started killing wolves. He was good at it. Every year he killed over five hundred of them. That came to more than five thousand dollars. It was quite a bit of money in those days.

After four or five years, Bill had killed so many wolves, there were hardly any left in that area. So he retired, and he vowed never to harm another wolf because wolves had made him rich.

Then one day a farmer reported that a white wolf had killed two of his sheep. He had shot at it and hit it, but the bullets didn't have any effect. Soon that wolf was seen all over the countryside, killing and running. But nobody could stop it.

One night it came into Bill's yard and killed his pet cow. Bill forgot about his decision never to harm another wolf. He went into town the next morning and bought a young lamb for bait. He took it out into the hills and tied it to a tree. Then he backed off about fifty yards and sat down under another tree. With his gun in his lap, he waited.

When Bill didn't come back, his friends started looking for him. Finally they found the lamb. It was still tied to a tree. It was hungry, but it was alive. Then they found Bill. He was still sitting against the other tree, but he was dead. His throat had been torn open.

But there was no sign of a struggle. His gun hadn't been fired. And there were no tracks in the soil around him. As for the white wolf, it was never seen again.

THE HAUNTED HOUSE

One time a preacher went to see if he could put a haunt to rest at a house in his settlement. The house had been haunted for about ten years. Several people had tried to stay there all night, but they always would get scared out by the haunt.

So this preacher took his Bible and went to the house—went on in, built himself a good fire, and lit a lamp. Sat there reading the Bible. Then just before midnight he heard something start up in the cellar—walking back and forth, back and forth. Then it sounded like somebody was trying to scream and got choked off. Then there was a lot of thrashing around and struggling, and finally everything got quiet.

The old preacher took up his Bible again, but before he could start reading, he heard footsteps coming up the cellar stairs. He sat watching the door to the cellar, and the footsteps kept coming closer and closer. He saw the doorknob turn, and when the door began to open, he jumped up and hollered, "What do you want?"

The door shut back easy-like, and there wasn't a sound. The preacher was trembling a little, but he finally opened the Bible and read awhile. Then he got up and laid the book on the chair and went to mending the fire.

Then the haunt started walking again and—step!—step!—step!—up the cellar stairs. The old preacher sat watching the door, saw the doorknob turn and the door open. It looked like a young woman. He backed up and said, "Who are you? What do you want?"

The haunt sort of swayed like she didn't know what to do—then she just faded out. The old preacher waited, waited, and when he didn't hear any more noises, he went over and shut the door. He was sweating and trembling all over, but he was a brave man and he thought he'd be able to see it through. So he turned his chair to where he could watch, and he sat down and waited.

It wasn't long before he heard the haunt start up again, slowly—step!—step!—step!—step!—closer, and closer—step!—step!—and it was right at the door.

The preacher stood up and held his Bible out before him. Then the knob slowly turned, and the door opened wide. This time the preacher spoke quiet-like. He said, "In the name of the Father, the Son, and the Holy Ghost—who are you and what do you want?"

The haunt came right across the room, straight to him, and took hold of his coat. It was a young woman about twenty years old. Her hair was torn and tangled, and the flesh was dropping off her face so he could see the bones and part of her teeth. She had no eyeballs, but there was a sort of blue light way back in her eye sockets. And she had no nose to her face.

Then she started talking. It sounded like her voice was coming and going with the wind blowing it. She told how her lover had killed her for her money and buried her in the cellar. She said if the preacher would dig up her bones and bury her properly, she could rest.

Then she told him to take the end joint of the little finger from her left hand, and to lay it in the collection plate at the next church meeting—and he'd find out who had murdered her.

And she said, "If you come back here once more after that—you'll hear my voice at midnight, and I'll tell you where my money is hid, and you can give it to the church."

The haunt sobbed like she was tired, and she sunk down toward the floor and was gone. The preacher found her bones and buried them in the graveyard.

The next Sunday the preacher put the finger bone in the collection plate, and when a certain man happened to touch it, it stuck to his hand. The man jumped up and rubbed and scraped and tore at that bone, trying to get it off. Then he went to screaming, like he was going crazy. Well, he confessed to the murder, and they took him on to jail.

After the man was hung, the preacher went back to that house one midnight, and the haunt's voice told him to dig under the hearthrock. He did, and he found a big sack of money. And where that haunt had held on to his coat, the print of those bony fingers was burned right into the cloth. It never did come out.

THE GUESTS

A young man and his wife were on a trip to visit his mother. Usually they arrived in time for supper. But they had gotten a late start, and now it was getting dark. So they decided to look for a place to stay overnight and go on in the morning.

Just off the road, they saw a small house in the woods. "Maybe they rent rooms," the wife said. So they stopped to ask.

An elderly man and woman came to the door. They

didn't rent rooms, they said. But they would be glad to have them stay overnight as their guests. They had plenty of room, and they would enjoy the company.

The old woman made coffee and brought out some cake, and the four of them talked for a while. Then the young couple were taken to their room. They again explained that they wanted to pay for this, but the old man said he would not accept any money.

The young couple got up early the next morning before their hosts had awakened. On a table near the front door, they left an envelope with some money in it for the room. Then they went on to the next town.

They stopped in a restaurant and had breakfast. When they told the owner where they had stayed, he was shocked.

"That can't be," he said. "That house burned to the ground, and the man and the woman who lived there died in the fire."

The young couple could not believe it. So they went back to the house. Only now there was no house. All they found was a burned-out shell.

They stood staring at the ruins trying to understand what had happened. Then the woman screamed. In the rubble was a badly burned table, like the one they had seen by the front door. On the table was the envelope they had left that morning.

THEY EAT
YOUR EYES,
THEY EAT
YOUR NOSE

*There are scary stories about
all kinds of things. The ones told
here are about a grave, a witch,
a man who liked to swim, a
hunting trip, and a market basket.
There also is one about worms
eating a corpse—your corpse.*

Don't you ev-er laugh as the hearse goes by, For
you may be— the next to die

THE HEARSE SONG

Don't you ever laugh as the hearse goes by,
For you may be the next to die.
They wrap you up in a big white sheet
From your head down to your feet.
They put you in a big black box
And cover you up with dirt and rocks.
All goes well for about a week,
Then your coffin begins to leak.
The worms crawl in, the worms crawl out,
The worms play pinochle on your snout.
They eat your eyes, they eat your nose,
They eat the jelly between your toes.
A big green worm with rolling eyes
Crawls in your stomach and out your eyes.
Your stomach turns a slimy green,
And pus pours out like whipping cream.
You spread it on a slice of bread,
And that's what you eat when you are dead.

THE GIRL WHO
STOOD ON A GRAVE

Some boys and girls were at a party one night. There was a graveyard down the street, and they were talking about how scary it was.

"Don't ever stand on a grave after dark," one of the boys said. "The person inside will grab you. He'll pull you under."

"That's not true," one of the girls said. "It's just a superstition."

"I'll give you a dollar if you stand on a grave," said the boy.

"A grave doesn't scare me," said the girl. "I'll do it right now."

The boy handed her his knife. "Stick this knife in one of the graves," he said. "Then we'll know you were there."

The graveyard was filled with shadows and was as quiet as death. "There is nothing to be scared of," the girl told herself, but she was scared anyway.

She picked out a grave and stood on it. Then quickly she bent over and plunged the knife into the soil, and she started to leave. But she couldn't get away. Something was holding her back! She tried a second time to leave, but she couldn't move. She was filled with terror.

"Something has got me!" she screamed, and she fell to the ground.

When she didn't come back, the others went to look for her. They found her body sprawled across the grave. Without realizing it, she had plunged the knife through her skirt and had pinned it to the ground. It was only the knife that held her. She had died of fright.

A NEW HORSE

Two farmhands shared a room. One slept at the back of the room. The other slept near the door. After a while, the one who slept near the door began to feel very tired early in the day. His friend asked what was wrong.

"An awful thing happens every night," he said. "A witch turns me into a horse and rides me all over the countryside."

"I'll sleep in your bed tonight," his friend said. "We'll see what happens to me."

About midnight an old woman who lived nearby came into the room. She mumbled some strange words over the farmhand, and he found he couldn't move. Then she slipped a bridle on him, and he turned into a horse.

The next thing he knew, she was riding him across the fields at breakneck speed, beating him to make him go even faster. Soon they came to a house where a party was going on. There was a lot of music and dancing. They were having a big time inside. She hitched him to a fence and went in.

While she was gone, the farmhand rubbed against the fence until the bridle came off, and he turned back into a human being.

Then he went into the house and found the witch. He spoke those strange words over her, and with the bridle he turned *her* into a horse. Then he rode her to a blacksmith and had her fitted with horseshoes. After that, he rode her to the farm where she lived.

"I have a pretty good filly here," he told her husband, "but I need a stronger horse. Would you like to trade?"

The old man looked her over, and he said he would do it. So they picked out another horse, and the farmhand rode away.

Her husband led his new horse to the barn. He took off the bridle and went to hang it up. But when he came back, the new horse was gone. Instead, there stood his wife with horseshoes nailed to her hands and feet.

ALLIGATORS

A young woman in town married a man from another part of the country. He was a nice fellow, and they got along pretty well together. There was only one problem. Every night he'd go swimming in the river. Sometimes he would be gone all night long, and she would complain about how lonely she was.

This couple had two young sons. As soon as the boys could walk, their father began to teach them how to swim. And when they got to be old enough, he took them swimming in the river at night. Often they would stay there all night long, and the young woman would stay home all by herself.

After a while, she began to act in a strange way— at least, that is what the neighbors said. She told them that her husband was turning into an alligator, and that he was trying to turn the boys into alligators.

Everybody told her there was nothing wrong with a man taking his sons swimming. That was a natural thing to do. And when it came to alligators, there just weren't any nearby. Everybody knew that.

Early one morning the young woman came running into town from the direction of the river. She was soaking wet. She said a big alligator and two little alligators had pulled her in and had tried to get her to eat a raw fish. They were her husband and her sons, she said, and they wanted her to live with them. But she had gotten away.

Her doctor decided she had lost her mind, and he had her put in the hospital for a while. After that nobody saw her husband and boys again. They just disappeared.

But now and then a fisherman would tell about seeing alligators in the river at night. Usually it was one big alligator and two small ones. But people said they were just making it up. Everybody knows there aren't any alligators around here.

ROOM FOR ONE MORE

A man named Joseph Blackwell came to Philadelphia on a business trip. He stayed with friends in the big house they owned outside the city. That night they had a good time visiting. But when Blackwell went to bed, he tossed and turned and couldn't sleep.

Sometime during the night he heard a car turn into the driveway. He went to the window to see who was arriving at such a late hour. In the moonlight, he saw a long, black hearse filled with people.

The driver of the hearse looked up at him. When Blackwell saw his queer, hideous face, he shuddered. The driver called to him, "There is room for one more." Then he waited for a minute or two, and he drove off.

In the morning Blackwell told his friends what had happened. "You were dreaming," they said.

"I must have been," he said, "but it didn't seem like a dream."

After breakfast he went into Philadelphia. He

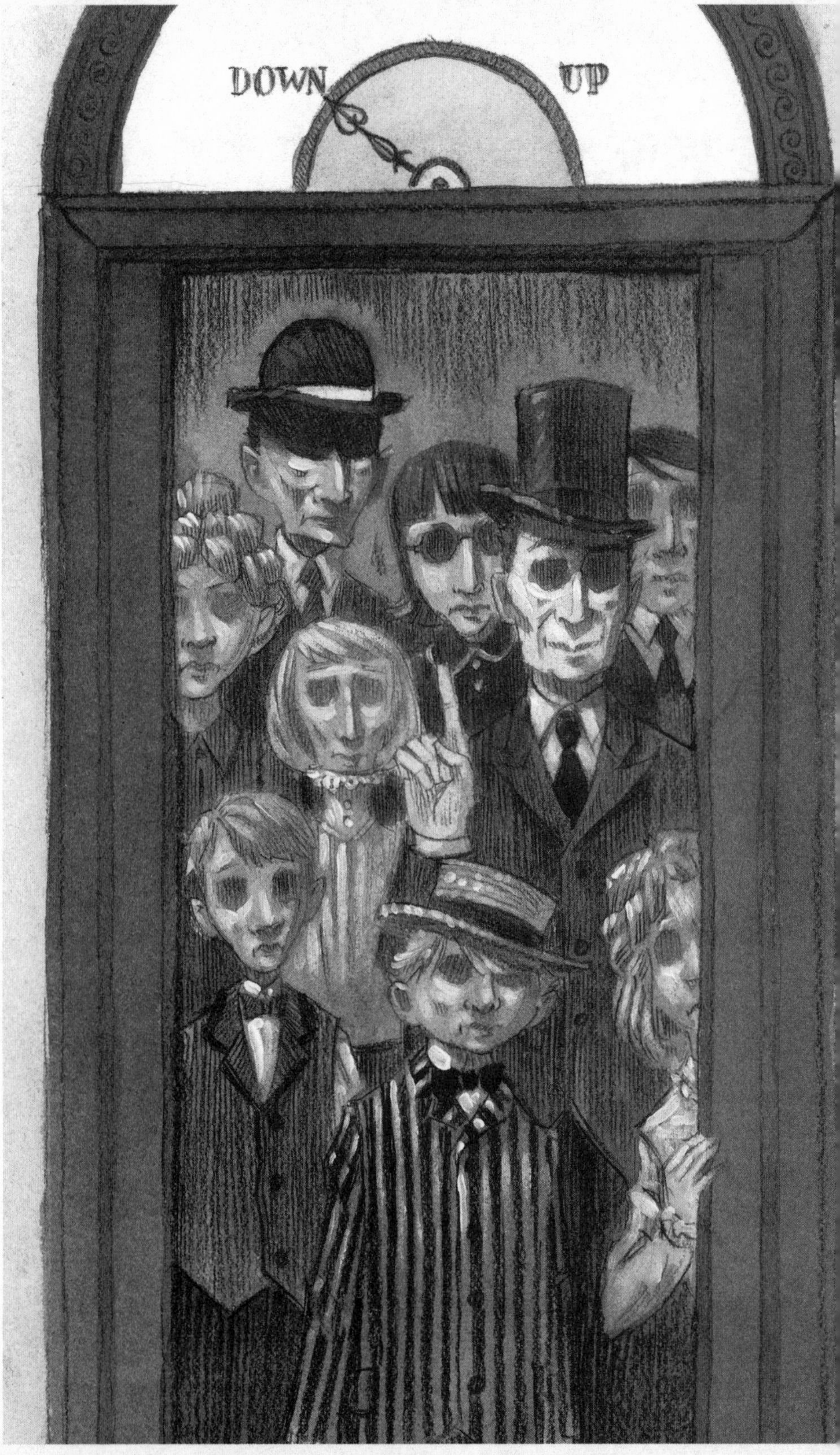
DOWN
UP

spent the day high above the city in one of the new office buildings there.

Late in the afternoon he was waiting for an elevator to take him back down to the street. But when it arrived, it was very crowded. One of the passengers looked out and called to him. "There is room for one more," he said. It was the driver of the hearse.

"No, thanks," said Blackwell. "I'll get the next one."

The doors closed, and the elevator started down. There was shrieking and screaming, then the sound of a crash. The elevator had fallen to the bottom of the shaft. Everyone aboard was killed.

THE WENDIGO

A wealthy man wanted to go hunting in a part of northern Canada where few people had ever hunted. He traveled to a trading post and tried to find a guide to take him. But no one would do it. It was too dangerous, they said.

Finally, he found an Indian who needed money badly, and he agreed to take him. The Indian's name was DéFago.

They made camp in the snow near a large frozen lake. For three days they hunted, but they had nothing to show for it. The third night a windstorm came up. They lay in their tent listening to the wind howling and the trees whipping back and forth.

To see the storm better, the hunter opened the tent flap. What he saw startled him. There wasn't a breath of air stirring, and the trees were standing perfectly still. Yet he could *hear* the wind howling. And the more he listened, the more it sounded as if it were calling DéFago's name.

"DA-FAAAAAAAAAY-GO!" it called. "DA-FAAAAAAAAAY-GO!"

"I must be losing my mind," the hunter thought.

But DéFago had gotten out of his sleeping bag. He was huddled in a corner of the tent, his head buried in his arms.

"What's this all about?" the hunter asked.

"It's nothing," DéFago said.

But the wind continued to call to him. And DéFago became more tense and more restless.

"DA-FAAAAAAAAAY-GO!" it called. "DA-FAAAAAAAAAY-GO!"

Suddenly, he jumped to his feet, and he began to run from the tent. But the hunter grabbed him and wrestled him to the ground.

"You can't leave me out here," the hunter shouted.

Then the wind called again, and DéFago broke loose and ran into the darkness. The hunter could hear him screaming as he went. Again and again he cried, "Oh, my fiery feet, my burning feet of fire . . ." Then his voice faded away, and the wind died down.

At daybreak, the hunter followed DéFago's tracks in the snow. They went through the woods, down toward the lake, then out onto the ice.

But soon he noticed something strange. The steps DéFago had taken got longer and longer. They were so long no human being could have taken them. It was as if something had helped him to hurry away.

The hunter followed the tracks out to the middle of the lake, but there they disappeared. At first, he thought that DéFago had fallen through the ice, but there wasn't any hole. Then he thought that something had pulled him off the ice into the sky. But that made no sense.

As he stood wondering what had happened, the wind picked up again. Soon it was howling as it had the night before. Then he heard DéFago's voice. It was coming from up above, and again he heard DéFago screaming, ". . . My fiery feet, my burning feet . . ." But there was nothing to be seen.

Now the hunter wanted to leave that place as fast as he could. He went back to camp and packed. Then he left some food for DéFago, and he started out. Weeks later he reached civilization.

The following year he went back to hunt in that area again. He went to the same trading post to look for a guide. The people there could not explain what had happened to DéFago that night. But they had not seen him since then.

"Maybe it was the Wendigo," one of them said, and he laughed. "It's supposed to come with the wind. It drags you along at great speed until your feet are burned away, and more of you than that. Then it carries you into the sky, and it drops you. It's just a crazy story, but that's what some of the Indians say."

A few days later the hunter was at the trading post again. An Indian came in and sat by the fire. He had a blanket wrapped around him, and he wore his hat so that you couldn't see his face. The hunter thought there was something familiar about him.

He walked over and he asked, "Are you DéFago?"

The Indian didn't answer.

"Do you know anything about him?"

No answer.

He began to wonder if something was wrong, if the man needed help. But he couldn't see his face.

"Are you all right?" he asked.

No answer.

To get a look at him, he lifted the Indian's hat. Then he screamed. There was nothing under the hat but a pile of ashes.

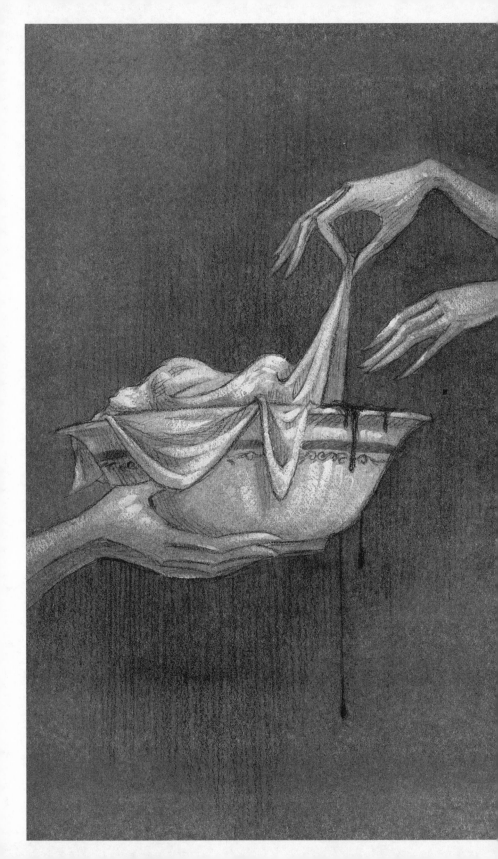

THE DEAD
MAN'S BRAINS

This scary story is a scary game that people play at Hallowe'en. But it can be played whenever the spirit moves you.

The players sit in a circle in a darkened room and listen to a storyteller describe the rotting remains of a corpse. Each part is passed around for them to feel.

In one version, a player is out if he or she screams or gasps with fright. In another version, everybody stays to the end, no matter how scared they get.

Here is the story:

Once in this town there lived a man named Brown. It was years ago, on this night, that he was murdered out of spite.

We have here his remains.

First, let's feel his brains. (A wet, squishy tomato)

Now here are his eyes, still frozen with surprise. (Two peeled grapes)

This is his nose. (A chicken bone)

Here is his ear. (A dried apricot)

And here is his hand, rotting flesh and bone. (A cloth or rubber glove filled with mud or ice)

But his hair still grows. (A handful of corn silk or wet fur or yarn)

And his heart still beats, now and then. (A piece of raw liver)

And his blood still flows. Dip your fingers in it. It's nice and warm. (A bowl of catsup thinned with warm water)

That's all there is, except for these worms. They are the ones that ate the rest of him. (A handful of wet, cooked spaghetti noodles)

"MAY I CARRY YOUR BASKET?"

Sam Lewis spent the evening playing chess at his friend's house. It was about midnight when they finished their game, and he started home. Outside it was icy cold and as quiet as the grave.

As he came around a turn in the road, he was surprised to see a woman walking ahead of him. She was carrying a basket covered with a white cloth. When he caught up to her, he looked to see who it was. But she was so bundled up against the cold, it was hard to see her face.

"Good evening," Sam said. "What brings you out so late?"

But she didn't answer.

Then he said, "May I carry your basket?"

She handed it to him. From under the cloth, a small voice said, "That's very nice of you," and that was followed by wild laughter.

Sam was so startled that he dropped the basket— and out rolled a woman's head. He looked at the head, and he stared at the woman. "It's *her* head!" he cried. And he started to run, and the woman and her head began to chase him.

Soon the head caught up to him. It bounded into the air and sunk its teeth into his left leg. Sam screamed with pain and ran faster.

But the woman and her head stayed right behind. Soon the head leaped into the air again and bit into his other leg. Then they were gone.

OTHER DANGERS

Most of the scary stories in this book
have been passed down over the years.
But the ones in this chapter have been told
only in recent times. They are stories that
young people often tell about dangers
we face in our lives today.

THE HOOK

Donald and Sarah went to the movies. Then they went for a ride in Donald's car. They parked up on a hill at the edge of town. From there they could see the lights up and down the valley.

Donald turned on the radio and found some music. But an announcer broke in with a news bulletin. A murderer had escaped from the state prison. He was armed with a knife and was headed south on foot. His left hand was missing. In its place, he wore a hook.

"Let's roll up the windows and lock the doors," said Sarah.

"That's a good idea," said Donald.

"That prison isn't too far away," said Sarah. "Maybe we really should go home."

"But it's only ten o'clock," said Donald.

"I don't care what time it is," she said. "I want to go home."

"Look, Sarah," said Donald, "he's not going to climb all the way up here. Why would he do that? Even if he did, all the doors are locked. How could he get in?"

"Donald, he could take that hook and break through a window and open a door," she said. "I'm scared. I want to go home."

Donald was annoyed. "Girls always are afraid of something," he said.

As he started the car, Sarah thought she heard someone, or something, scratching at her door.

"Did you hear that?" she asked as they roared away. "It sounded like somebody was trying to get in."

"Oh, sure," said Donald.

Soon they got to her house.

"Would you like to come in and have some cocoa?" she asked.

"No," he said, "I've got to go home."

He went around to the other side of the car to let her out. Hanging on the door handle was a hook.

THE WHITE SATIN
EVENING GOWN

A young man invited a young woman to a formal dance. But she was very poor, and she could not afford to buy the evening gown she needed for such an occasion.

"Maybe you can rent a dress," her mother said. So she went to a pawnshop not far from where she lived. There she found a white satin evening gown in her size. She looked lovely in it, and she was able to rent it for very little.

When she arrived at the dance with her friend, she was so attractive, everyone wanted to meet her. She danced again and again and was having a wonderful time. But then she began to feel dizzy and faint, and she asked her friend to take her home. "I think I have danced too much," she told him.

When she got home, she lay down on her bed. The next morning her mother found that her daughter had died. The doctor did not understand what had caused her death. So he had the coroner perform an autopsy.

The coroner found that she had been poisoned by embalming fluid. It had stopped her blood from flowing. There were traces of the fluid on her dress. He decided it had entered her skin when she perspired while she was dancing.

The pawnbroker said he bought the dress from an undertaker's helper. It had been used in a funeral for another young woman, and the helper had stolen it just before she was buried.

HIGH BEAMS

The girl driving the old blue sedan was a senior at the high school. She lived on a farm about eight miles away and used the car to drive back and forth.

She had driven into town that night to see a basketball game. Now she was on her way home. As she pulled away from the school, she noticed a red pickup truck follow her out of the parking lot. A few minutes later the truck was still behind her.

"I guess we're going in the same direction," she thought.

She began to watch the truck in her mirror. When she changed her speed, the driver of the truck changed his speed. When she passed a car, so did he.

Then he turned on his high beams, flooding her car with light. He left them on for almost a minute. "He probably wants to pass me," she thought. But she was becoming uneasy.

Usually she drove home over a back road. Not too many people went that way. But when she turned onto that road, so did the truck.

"I've got to get away from him," she thought, and she began to drive faster. Then he turned his high beams on again. After a minute, he turned them off. Then he turned them on again and off again.

She drove even faster, but the truck driver stayed right behind her. Then he turned his high beams on again. Once more her car was ablaze with light. "What is he doing?" she wondered. "What *does* he want?" Then he turned them off again. But a minute later he had them on again, and he left them on.

At last she pulled into her driveway, and the truck pulled in right behind her. She jumped from the car and ran to the house. "Call the police!" she screamed at her father. Out in the driveway she could see the driver of the truck. He had a gun in his hand.

When the police arrived, they started to arrest him, but he pointed to the girl's car. "You don't want me," he said. "You want him."

Crouched behind the driver's seat, there was a man with a knife.

As the driver of the truck explained it, the man slipped into the girl's car just before she left the school. He saw it happen, but there was no way he could stop it. He thought about getting the police, but he was afraid to leave her. So he followed her car.

Each time the man in the back seat reached up to overpower her, the driver of the truck turned on his high beams. Then the man dropped down, afraid that someone might see him.

THE BABYSITTER

It was nine o'clock in the evening. Everybody was sitting on the couch in front of the TV. There were Richard, Brian, Jenny, and Doreen, the babysitter.

The telephone rang.

"Maybe it's your mother," said Doreen. She picked up the phone. Before she could say a word, a man laughed hysterically and hung up.

"Who was it?" asked Richard.

"Some nut," said Doreen. "What did I miss?"

At nine-thirty the telephone rang again. Doreen answered it. It was the man who had called before. "I'll be there soon," he said, and he laughed and hung up.

"Who was it?" the children asked.

"Some crazy person," she said.

About ten o'clock the telephone rang again. Jenny got to it first.

"Hello," she said.

It was the same man. "One more hour," he said, and he laughed and hung up.

"He said, 'One more hour.' What did he mean?" asked Jenny.

"Don't worry," said Doreen. "It's somebody fooling around."

"I'm scared," said Jenny.

About ten-thirty the telephone rang once more. When Doreen picked it up, the man said, "Pretty soon now," and he laughed.

"*Why* are you doing this?" Doreen screamed, and he hung up.

"Was it that guy again?" asked Brian.

"Yes," said Doreen. "I'm going to call the operator and complain."

The operator told her to call back if it happened again, and she would try to trace the call.

At eleven o'clock the telephone rang again. Doreen answered it. "Very soon now," the man said, and he laughed and hung up.

Doreen called the operator. Almost at once she called back. "That person is calling from a telephone upstairs," she said. "You'd better leave. I'll get the police."

Just then a door upstairs opened. A man they had never seen before started down the stairs toward them. As they ran from the house, he was smiling in a very strange way. A few minutes later, the police found him there and arrested him.

"AAAAAAAAAAAH!"

*This chapter has the same title as the
first chapter. But the stories in the first chapter
are meant to scare you. The ones in this chapter
are meant to make you laugh.*

THE VIPER

A widow lived alone on the top floor of an apartment house. One morning her telephone rang.

"Hello," she said.

"This is the viper," a man said. "I'm coming up."

"Somebody is fooling around," she thought, and hung up.

A half hour later the telephone rang again. It was the same man.

"It's the viper," he said. "I'll be up soon."

The widow didn't know what to think, but she was getting frightened.

Once more the telephone rang. Again it was the viper.

"I'm coming up now," he said.

She quickly called the police. They said they would be right over. When the doorbell rang, she sighed with relief. "They are here!" she thought.

But when she opened the door, there stood a little old man with a bucket and a cloth. "I am the viper," he said. "I vish to vash and vipe the vindows."

THE ATTIC

A man named Rupert lived with his dog in a house deep in the woods. Rupert was a hunter and a trapper. The dog was a big German shepherd named Sam. Rupert had raised Sam from a pup.

Almost every morning Rupert went hunting, and Sam stayed behind and guarded the house. One morning, as Rupert was checking his traps, he got the feeling that something was wrong at home.

He hurried back as fast as he could, but when he got there he found that Sam was missing. He searched the house and the woods nearby, but Sam was nowhere to be seen. He called and he called, but the dog did not answer. For days Rupert looked for Sam, but he could find no trace of him.

Finally he gave up and went back to his work. But one morning he heard something moving in the attic. He picked up his gun. Then he thought, "I'd better be quiet about this."

So he took off his boots. And in his bare feet he

began to climb the attic stairs. He slowly took one step—then another—then another, until at last he reached the attic door.

He stood outside listening, but he didn't hear a thing. Then he opened the door, and—

"AAAAAAAAAAAH!"

(At this point, the storyteller stops, as if he has finished. Then usually somebody will ask, "Why did Rupert scream?"

The storyteller replies, "You'd scream too if you stepped on a nail in your bare feet.")

THE SLITHERY-DEE

The slithery-dee,
He came out of the sea;

He ate all the others,
But he didn't eat me.

The slithery-dee,
He came out of the sea;

He ate all the others,
But he didn't eat—

SL-U-R-P . . .

AARON KELLY'S
BONES

Aaron Kelly was dead. They bought him a coffin and had a funeral and buried him.

But that night he got out of his coffin, and he came home. His family was sitting around the fire when he walked in.

He sat down next to his widow, and he said, "What's going on? You all act like somebody died. Who's dead?"

His widow said, "You are."

"I don't feel dead," he said. "I feel fine."

"You don't look fine," his widow said. "You look dead. You'd better get back to the grave where you belong."

"I'm not going back to the grave until I *feel* dead," he said.

Since Aaron wouldn't go back, his widow couldn't collect his life insurance. Without that, she couldn't pay for the coffin. And the undertaker said he would take it back.

Aaron didn't care. He just sat by the fire rocking in a chair and warming his hands and feet. But his joints were dry and his back was stiff, and every time he moved, he creaked and cracked.

One night the best fiddler in town came to court the widow. Since Aaron was dead, the fiddler wanted to marry her. The two of them sat on one side of the fire, and Aaron sat on the other side, creaking and cracking.

"How long do we have to put up with this dead corpse?" the widow asked.

"Something must be done," the fiddler said.

"This isn't very jolly," Aaron said. "Let's dance!"

The fiddler got out his fiddle and began to play. Aaron stretched himself, shook himself, got up, took a step or two, and began to dance.

With his old bones rattling, and his yellow teeth snapping, and his bald head wagging, and his arms flip-flopping—around and around he went.

With his long legs clicking, and his kneebones knocking, he skipped and pranced around the room. How that dead man danced! But pretty soon a bone worked loose and fell to the floor.

"Look at that!" said the fiddler.

"Play faster!" said the widow.

The fiddler played faster.

Crickety-crack, down and back, the dead man went hopping, and his dry bones kept dropping—this way, that way, the pieces just kept popping.

"Play, man! Play!" cried the widow.

The fiddler fiddled, and dead Aaron danced. Then Aaron fell apart, collapsed into a pile of bones—all except his bald headbone *that* grinned at the fiddler, cracked its teeth—and kept dancing.

"Look at that!" groaned the fiddler.

"Play louder!" cried the widow.

"Ho, ho!" said the headbone. "Ain't we having fun!"

The fiddler couldn't stand it. "Widow," he said. "I'm going home," and he never came back.

The family gathered up Aaron's bones and put them back in the coffin. They mixed them up so he couldn't fit them together. After that, Aaron stayed in his grave.

But his widow never did get married again. Aaron had seen to that.

WAIT TILL MARTIN COMES

An old man was out for a walk. When a storm came up, he looked for a place to take shelter. Soon he came to an old house. He ran up on the porch and knocked on the door, but nobody answered.

By now rain was pouring down, thunder was booming, and lightning was flashing. So he tried the door. When he found it was unlocked, he went inside.

Except for a pile of wooden boxes, the house was empty. He broke up some of the boxes and made a fire with them. Then he sat down in front of the fire and dried himself. It was so warm and cozy that he fell asleep.

When he woke up a black cat was sitting near the fire. It stared at him for a while. Then it purred. "That's a nice cat," he thought, and he dozed off again.

When he opened his eyes, there was a second cat in the room. But this one was as big as a wolf. It looked at him very closely, and it asked, "Shall we do it now?"

"No," said the other cat. "Let's wait till Martin comes."

"I must be dreaming," thought the old man. He closed his eyes again. Then he took another look. But now there was as a *third* cat in the room, and this one was as big as a tiger. It looked the old man over, and it asked, "Shall we do it now?"

"No," said the others. "Let's wait till Martin comes."

The old man jumped up, jumped out the window and started running. "When Martin comes, you tell him I couldn't wait," he called.

THE GHOST
WITH THE
BLOODY FINGERS

A businessman arrived at a hotel late one night and asked for a room. The room clerk told him the hotel was all filled up. "There is only one empty room," he said. "But we don't rent that one because it is haunted."

"I'll take it," said the businessman. "I don't believe in ghosts."

The man went up to the room. He unpacked his things, and he went to bed. As soon as he did, a ghost came out of the closet. Its fingers were bleeding, and it was moaning, "Bloody fingers! Bloody fingers!" When the man saw the ghost, he grabbed his things and ran.

The next night a woman arrived very late. Again, all the rooms were taken except the haunted room.

"I'll sleep there," she said. "I'm not afraid of ghosts."

As soon as she got into bed, the ghost came out of the closet. Its fingers still were bleeding. It still was moaning, "Bloody fingers! Bloody fingers!" And the woman took one look and ran.

A week later another guest arrived very late. He also took the haunted room.

After he unpacked, he got out his guitar and he began to play. Soon the ghost appeared. As before, its fingers were bleeding, and it was moaning, "Bloody fingers! Bloody fingers!"

The man paid no attention. He just kept strumming his guitar. But the ghost kept moaning, and its fingers kept bleeding.

Finally, the guitar player looked up. "Cool it, man!" he said. "Get yourself a Band-Aid."

ABBREVIATIONS IN NOTES, SOURCES, AND BIBLIOGRAPHY

CFQ   *California Folklore Quarterly*

HF   *Hoosier Folklore*

HFB   *Hoosier Folklore Bulletin*

IF   *Indiana Folklore*

JAF   *Journal of American Folklore*

KFQ   *Kentucky Folklore Quarterly*

MFA   Maryland Folklore Archive, University of Maryland, College Park, Md.

NEF   *Northeast Folklore*

NMFR   *New Mexico Folklore Record*

NYFQ   *New York Folklore Quarterly*

PTFS   Publication of the Texas Folklore Society

RU   Compiler's collection of folklore, contributed by his students at Rutgers University, New Brunswick, N.J., 1963–78.

SFQ	*Southern Folklore Quarterly*
UMFA	University of Massachusetts Folklore Archive, Amherst, Mass.
WSFA	Wayne State University Folklore Archive, Detroit, Mich.

NOTES

The publications cited are described in the Bibliography.

Jump stories (pp. 5–20): There are dozens of jump stories, but today only two are widely known. One is "The Big Toe," which appears in Chapter 1 and circulates in southeastern United States. The other is "The Golden Arm," from which "The Big Toe" derives.

In "The Golden Arm," a man marries a woman who wears a beautifully crafted golden arm. When she dies, he steals it from her grave, only to have her ghost return to claim it. In some variants, it is a golden heart he steals or golden hair or diamond eyes. Or it is a natural organ, usually the liver or the heart, that he eats, despite the cannibalism involved.

"The Big Toe" is an American tale. "The Golden Arm," although widely used in the United States, has English and German antecedents. The Grimm brothers reported a version of it early in the nineteenth century, but the tale predates that period.

Mark Twain used to tell "The Golden Arm" in his public performances. Here is some advice he once gave on delivering the jump lines that he once gave. It also applies to the telling of "The Big Toe."

"You must wail ['Who's got my golden arm?'] very plaintively and accusingly; then you [pause, and you] stare steadily and impressively into the face of . . . a girl, preferably—and let that awe-inspiring pause build into a deep hush. When it has reached exactly the right length, jump suddenly at that girl and yell, 'You've got it!'

"If you got your pause right, she'll fetch a dear little yelp and spring right out of her shoes. . . ."

There are three approaches to telling these jump stories. Two are found in Chapter 1. In the third approach, the ghost returns to search for what has been stolen. Feigning innocence, the grave robber asks what has become of various parts of the ghost's body. To each question, the ghost replies, "All withered and wasted away." When the robber mentions the part of the body that was stolen, the ghost shrieks, "You've got it!" See Botkin, *American*, pp. 502–503; Burrison; Roberts, *Old Greasybeard*, pp. 33–36; Stimson, *JAF* 58:126.

Ghosts (pp. 21–36): In almost every civilization, there has been a belief that the dead return. They are said to come back for various reasons. Their lives were ended before their "allotted time." They did not receive a proper burial. They had important business to finish or a responsibility to meet. They wished to punish somebody or to take revenge. Or they wanted to comfort or advise someone, or obtain forgiveness.

It is said that some return as human beings. In fact, they may look just as they did when they were alive, and people they meet may not realize they are ghosts.

One of the best known of these "living ghosts" is the ghostly or vanishing hitchhiker. It usually is late at night that a motorist encounters her. She is standing on a street corner or at the side of a road, and she asks to be taken home.

She sits in the back seat of the car. But when the driver finds the address he has been given, he discovers that she has vanished. When he informs her family of this, he learns that she died on that night several years before at the spot where he picked her up.

There are two stories about living ghosts in Chapter 2: "The Guests" and "Cold as Clay."

Some persons who die are said to return as animals, particularly as dogs. Other ghosts may have a spectral quality. Or they may appear as a ball of fire or as a moving light. Or they may make their presence known through sounds they make or actions they take, such as slamming a door, rattling a key in a lock, or moving furniture.

The ghosts of animals also have been reported, as have the ghosts of objects such as guns, boots, and rifles, and trains and cars associated with death.

Ghosts of human beings do many things a human does. They eat, drink, ride on trains and buses, play the piano, and go fishing. They also laugh, cry, shout, whisper, and make all sorts of noises.

When it has completed what it set out to do, a ghost is likely to return to its grave. But at times this may require the help of a person, such as a minister, who may be experienced in "laying" ghosts, or putting them to rest.

If you wish to see or hear a ghost, these are some recommended approaches: Look back over your left shoulder. Look through either one of a mule's ears. Look in a mirror with another person. Arrange six pure white dinner plates around a table, then go to a cemetery at noon and call the name of someone you once knew who is buried there.

If you encounter a ghost, it is advised that you speak

to it. If you do so, you may be able to help it finish whatever it is doing and return to its grave. Some say it is most effective if you address a ghost this way: "In the name of God [or in the name of the Father, the Son, and the Holy Ghost], what do you want?" They also say that holding a Bible will protect you against a revengeful ghost and demonstrate your sincerity.

However, most ghosts are not regarded as dangerous. As the folklorist Maria Leach pointed out, "Usually a ghost is some poor harmless soul . . . looking for someone with enough understanding and kindness to speak to it and do it some little favor." See Beardsley and Hankie, *CFQ* 1:303–36; *CFQ* 2:3–25; Creighton, pp. i–xi; Hole, pp. 1–12; Gardner, p. 85; Leach, *Dictionary*, "Revenant," pp. 933–34; Leach, *Thing*, pp. 9–11.

"The Thing" (pp. 22–23): This tale describes a forerunner, or a forewarning of death. The warning is a skeletonlike figure that appears, then chases the principal characters. The skeleton actually is a "wraith," an apparition that depicts a living person as he or she will look at death. But the most commonly reported forerunners are heard, not seen. They are sounds like a knock on the door or the striking of a clock. See Creighton, pp. 1–7, 69–70.

"The Haunted House" (pp. 31–34): The tale of a person who is brave enough to spend a night in a haunted house, and who often is rewarded for his bravery, is told again and again around the world. There are many versions of this story, but the theme never changes. In this book there are four disparate variants of this tale: "Me Tie Dough-ty Walker!" "The Haunted House," "Wait till Martin Comes," and "The Ghost with the Bloody Fingers." The tale is classified as Type 326 (the youth

who wanted to know what fear was). See Ives, *NEF* 4:61–
67; Roberts, *Old Greasybeard*, pp. 72–74, 187; Roberts,
South, pp. 35–38, 217–18.

"The Hearse Song" (p. 39): Although many adults are
familiar with this song, it is best known in the elementary
schools. But during World War I, it was a war song that
was sung by servicemen from America and England. One
version went this way:

> Did you ever think as the hearse rolls by
> That some of these days you must surely die?
> They'll take you away in a big black hack;
> They'll take you away but they won't bring you back.
>
> And your eyes drop out and your teeth fall in
> And the worms crawl over your mouth and chin;
> And the worms crawl out and the worms crawl in
> And your limbs drop off limb by limb.

The words have changed quite a bit since then. Worms
now play pinochle on your snout. There is jelly between
your toes. And pus, like whipping cream, pours out of
your stomach.

With children as the audience, it is a more gruesome
song, but it is not as grim. One scholar associates the
change of words with a change of function. During World
War I, the song helped servicemen deal with the fear they
felt. These days it helps children confirm the reality of
death, yet through satire and humor deny its reality for
them.

The song is part of an old poetic tradition. During
the Middle Ages many of the poems written in European

countries dealt with death and decay. Here is a verse of this type from a twelfth-century poem, which has been translated from the Middle English:

A vicious worm lives in my backbone;
My eyes are dazed and very dim;
My guts rot, my hair is green,
My teeth grin very grimly.

At that time such poems may have served still another purpose: turning one's thoughts from the flesh to the hereafter. See Doyle, PTFS 40:175–90; for two World War I versions of "The Hearse Song," see Sandburg, p. 444.

"*The Wendigo*" (pp. 50–53): The Wendigo, or Windigo, is a female spirit that personifies the awful cold of the northern forests. She figures in the folklore of forest Indians in Canada and in sections of northernmost United States.

According to this legend, the Wendigo attracts victims by calling to them in an irresistible way, then bears them away at great speed, finally sweeps them into the sky, then drops them, leaving them with frozen stumps where their feet once were. As they are carried off, they characteristically scream, ". . . My fiery feet, my burning feet of fire!"

The only defense against the Wendigo is to restrain the person who is being called. But the spirit then tries to entice whoever is holding him. See Crowe, *NMFR* 11:22–23.

In the lore of some northern tribes, the Wendigo functions not as the spirit of the cold, but as a cannibal giant that kills for human flesh. Some nineteenth-century

Indians also suffered a compulsion to eat human flesh, an illness anthropologists later described as a "Windigo psychosis." See Speck, *JAF* 48:81–82; Brown, *American Anthropologist* 73:20–21.

Belief legends (pp. 59–70): The stories in Chapter 4 are not hard to believe. They deal with ordinary people. They describe incidents that do not seem beyond the realm of possibility.

But the same incidents are reported again and again at locations in different parts of the country. And it is never possible to trace these stories to the actual participants. The closest one usually comes is a report from someone who knew someone who knew those involved.

(The one known exception involves the legend of a "death car," a late model automobile that was sold for virtually nothing because of the smell of a corpse that cannot be removed. The folklorist Richard M. Dorson traced the origins of the story to Mecosta, Michigan, where the incident occurred in 1938.)

Most of these stories are expressions of the anxiety people have about certain aspects of their lives. They evolve from incidents and rumors that reinforce these fears, and around which stories are constructed.

These modern legends are described by folklorists as "migratory belief legends." They are "migratory" in the sense that they do not attach themselves to single locations, as traditional legends often do. They are among the most vigorous of modern folklorist forms.

All the stories in Chapter 4 are belief legends about some of the dangers that might confront a young person. The story "Room for One More," in Chapter 3, is another belief legend. It is concerned with the supernatural, but it has been reported in several locations in the United States and the British Isles.

These legends also are concerned with violence, horror, threats posed by technology, impurity of food, relationships with friends and relatives, personal embarrassment, and other sources of anxiety.

They circulate by word of mouth, but at times the media carry reports that further disseminate them. See Brunvand, *American*, pp. 110–12; Brunvand, *Urban American Legends*; Dégh, "'Belief Legend,'" pp. 56–68.

"The White Satin Evening Gown" (p. 63–64): Two versions of this story were known in ancient Greece. Hercules dies when he wears a robe his wife poisoned with the blood of his rival, the centaur Nessus. Medea sends a gift of a poisoned robe to Creusa, the woman her former husband, Jason, intends to marry. When Creusa tries on the robe, she dies. See Himelick, *HF* 5:83–84.

SOURCES

The source of each item is given, along with variants and related information. Where available, the names of collectors (C) and informants (I) are given. Publications cited are described in the Bibliography.

Strange and Scary Things

p. 2   *"There was a man dwelt . . .":* Prince Mamillius begins to tell his tale in Act II, Scene 1, of *The Winter's Tale.* The lines quoted have been rearranged slightly for clarity. See Shakespeare, p. 1107.

1. *"Aaaaaaaaaaah!"*

p. 7   *"The Big Toe:"* These are variants of "The Big Toe," a traditional story which is widespread in southern United States. I learned them while serving in the U.S. Navy during World War II. My informant was a sailor from either Virginia or West Virginia. The tales are retold from memory. For parallels, see Boggs, *JAF* 47:296; Chase, *American,* pp. 57–59; Chase, *Grandfather,* pp. 22–26; Kennedy, PTFS 6:41–42; Roberts, *South,* pp. 52–54.

p. 10   *"The Walk":* (I) Edward Knowlton, Stonington, Maine, 1976. For a parallel, see "Ma Uncle Sandy," a

Scottish tale that ends with the jump word "WOW!" in Briggs, *Dictionary*, Part A, vol. 2, p. 542.

p. 13   *"What Do You Come For?"*: This is a retelling of a tale told in America and in the British Isles. See Bacon, *JAF* 35:290; Boggs, *JAF* 47:296–97. For a nineteenth-century Scottish version, "The Strange Visitor," see Chambers, pp. 64–65.

p. 14   *"Me Tie Dough-ty Walker!"*: This is a retelling of a Kentucky tale collected by Herbert Halpert in Bloomington, Indiana, in 1940. The informant was Mrs. Otis Milby Melcher. For Dr. Halpert's transcription of the tale and an interview with the informant, see *HFB* 1:9–11. The story appears under the title "The Rash Dog and the Bloody Head." It has been expanded slightly, in line with the informant's published suggestions for telling. The ending also has been modified slightly. In the original ending, the storyteller pauses after the dog dies, then shouts "BOO!" Several children who heard the story didn't think the ending was scary enough. Bill Tucker, twelve, and Billy Green, twelve, of Bangor, Maine, suggested the change. Motif: H. 1411.1 (fear test: staying in a haunted house where a corpse drops piecemeal down the chimney). For related haunted house tales, see Boggs, *JAF* 47:296–97; Ives, *NEF* 4:61–67; Randolph, *Turtle*, pp. 22–23; Roberts, *South*, pp. 35–38. In this book, see "The Haunted House," pp. 31–34.

p. 17   *"A Man Who Lived in Leeds"*: (I) Tom O'Brien, San Francisco, 1975. The informant learned this from his English father around the turn of the century. For an English parallel, see Blakesborough, p. 258.

p. 19   *"Old Woman All Skin and Bone"*: A traditional song and tale in America and the British Isles. For variants, see Belden, pp. 502–503; Chase, *American*, p. 186; Cox, *FolkSongs*, pp. 482–83; Flanders, 180–81; Stimson, *JAF* 58:126.

2. He Heard Footsteps Coming
Up the Cellar Stairs. . .

p. 22   *"The Thing"*: This tale of a forerunner of death is based on an account in Helen Creighton's book, *Bluenose Ghosts*, pp. 4–6.

p. 25   *"Cold as Clay"*: This is a tale told both in America and England. It is based on the English ballad "The Suffolk Miracle." See Child, vol. 5, no. 272, p. 66. For a text of the tale as it was told in Virginia, see Gainer, pp. 62–63. Motif: E.210 (dead lover's malevolent return).

p. 27   *"The White Wolf"*: This is a retelling of an incident reported by Ruth Ann Musick in *The Telltale Lilac Bush and Other West Virginia Ghost Stories*, pp. 134–35. (I) Lester Tinnell, French Creek, West Virginia, 1954. Motifs: E.423.2.7 (revenant as wolf); E.320 (return from dead to inflict punishment).

p. 31   *"The Haunted House"*: This story was reported by Richard Chase in *American Folk Tales and Songs*, pp. 60–63. He collected it in Wise County, Virginia, prior to 1956. Abridged slightly for clarity.

p. 35   *"The Guests"*: This story has been told in many places. At one time it was well known in the area around Albany, New York. The version in this book is based on two sources: the recollection of my wife, Barbara Carmer Schwartz, who grew up in the Albany area, and an account reported by Louis C. Jones in *Things That Go Bump in the Night*, pp. 76–78. Dr. Jones's informant was Sunna Cooper.

3. They Eat Your Eyes, They Eat Your Nose

p. 39   *"The Hearse Song"*: Variant of a traditional song, Brooklyn, New York, 1940s. For a compilation of variants, see Doyle, PTFS 40:175–90.

p. 40   *"The Girl Who Stood on a Grave"*: This is a retelling of an old tale that is well known in America and the British Isles. In other versions, the victim is pinned by a stick, a post, a croquet stake, a sword, and a fork. See Boggs, *JAF* 47:295–96; Roberts, *South*, 136–37; Montell, 200–201. Motifs: H.1416.1 (fear test: visiting a graveyard at night); N. 334 (accidental fatal ending of game or joke).

p. 43   *"A New Horse"*: This witch tale has been told all over the world. The retelling in this book is based on a tale from the Kentucky mountains reported by Leonard Roberts. In that version the old man takes a gun and blows his wife's brains out after he realizes she is a witch. See Roberts, *Up Cutshin*, pp. 128–29.

p. 45   *"Alligators"*: This story is based on an Ozark tale Vance Randolph reported as "The Alligator Story" in *Sticks in the Knapsack*, pp. 22–23. He collected it from an elderly woman at Willow Springs, Missouri, in August 1939.

p. 47   *"Room for One More"*: RU, 1970. This legend has circulated for many years in the United States and the British Isles. For two English versions, see Briggs, *Dictionary*, vol. 2, pp. 545–46, 575-76.

p. 50   *"The Wendigo"*: This Indian tale also is a summer camp tale that is well known in northeastern United States. It is adapted from a version that Professor Edward

M. Ives of the University of Maine narrated for me. He first heard it in the 1930s when he attended Camp Curtis Read, a Boy Scout camp near Mahopac, New York. For a literary version of this tale, see "The Wendigo" by the English author Algernon Blackwood, in Davenport, pp. 1–58. The name DéFago used in the above adaptation is taken from this story.

p. 55   *"The Dead Man's Brains"*: The first paragraph of the story, MFA, 1975. The rest is so widely known, it is not based on any particular version.

p. 57   *"May I Carry Your Basket?"*: (I) Tom O'Brien, San Francisco, 1976. This is a bogeyman story the informant learned from his English father around the turn of the century. For a close variant, see Briggs, *Dictionary*, vol. 1, p. 500. Also see Nuttall, *JAF* 8:122, for a reference to an ancient Mexican Indian tale of a human skull that chases passersby, stops when they stop, runs when they run.

4. *Other Dangers*

p. 60   *"The Hook"*: This legend is so well known, particularly on college campuses, that this telling is not based on any particular variant. For parallels, see Barnes, *SFQ* 30:310; Emrich, p. 333; Fouke, p. 263; Parochetti, *KFQ* 10:49; Thigpen, *IF* 4:183–86.

p. 63   *"The White Satin Evening Gown"*: This tale has been reported in several sections of the United States, particularly the Midwest. The retelling is based on a number of variants. See Halpert, *HFB* 4:19–20, 32–34; Reaver, *NYFQ* 8:217–20.

p. 65   *"High Beams"*: This retelling is based on a report by Carlos Drake in *IF* 1:107–109. For parallels, see Cord, *IF* 2:49–52; Parochetti, *KFQ* 10:47–49. In a variant I collected in Waverly, Iowa, a woman stops for gasoline at a service station in a rundown neighborhood. The attendant notices a man hiding in the back seat. He takes the woman's money, but does not return with her change. After waiting several minutes, she goes inside for her money. The attendant then tells her about the man, and she calls the police.

p. 69   *"The Babysitter"*: (I) Jeff Rosen, sixteen, Jenkintown, Pennsylvania, 1980. In a widespread version, the intruder is captured by the police after the children are found murdered in their beds. The sitter escapes. See Fouke, p. 264. An American film based on this theme, *When a Stranger Calls*, was released in 1979.

5. *"Aaaaaaaaaaah!"*

p. 72   *"The Viper"*: (I) Leslie Kush, fourteen, Philadelphia, 1980. For a parallel, see Knapp, p. 247.

p. 74   *"The Attic"*: Compiler's recollection. In a variant, the hunter has two children who disappear. He decides to look for them in the attic, then screams when he opens the door. See Leach, *Rainbow*, pp. 218–19.

p. 77   *"The Slithery-Dee"*: UMFA, (C) Andrea Lagoy; (I) Jackie Lagoy, Leominster, Massachusetts, 1972.

p. 79   *"Aaron Kelly's Bones"*: This story is a retelling of a tale collected along the South Carolina coast prior to 1943. The collector was John Bennett. He reported the tale with the title "Daid Aaron II," in *The Doctor to the Dead*, pp. 249–52. His informants were Sarah Rutledge and Epsie Meggett, two black women who told the story in the Gullah dialect. Motif: E.410 (the unquiet grave).

p. 82   *"Wait till Martin Comes"*: Retelling of a traditional Negro folk tale that has circulated in southeastern United States. In some versions the cat waits for "Emmett," "Patience," or "Whalem-Balem," instead of Martin. See Pucket, p. 132; Cox, *JAF* 47:352–55; Fauset, *JAF* 40:258–59; Botkin, *American*, p. 711.

p. 85   *"The Ghost with the Bloody Fingers"*: WSFA, (C) Ramona Martin, 1973. In a variant, the ghost is a monster that kills everyone who occupies a haunted hotel room, except for a hippie who plays the guitar. See Vlach, *IF* 4:100–101.

BIBLIOGRAPHY

Books

Books that may be of interest to young people are marked with an asterisk (*).

Beck, Horace P. *The Folklore of Maine*. Philadelphia: J. B. Lippincott Co., 1957.

Belden, Henry M. *Ballads and Songs Collected by the Missouri FolkLore Society*, vol. 15. Columbia, Mo.: University of Missouri, 1940.

Bennett, John. *The Doctor to the Dead: Grotesque Legends & Folk Tales of Old Charleston*. New York: Rinehart & Co., 1943.

Bett, Henry. *English Legends*. London: B. T. Batsford, 1952.

Blackwood, Algernon. "The Wendigo." In Basil Davenport, *Ghostly Stories to Be Told*. New York: Dodd, Mead & Co., 1950.

Blakeborough, Richard. *Wit, Character, Folklore & Customs of the North Riding of Yorkshire*. Salisbury-by-the-Sea, England: W. Rapp & Sons, 1911.

Bontemps, Arna, and Langston Hughes. *The Book of Negro Folklore*. New York: Dodd, Mead & Co., 1958.

Botkin, Benjamin A., ed. *A Treasury of American Folklore*. New York: Crown Publishers, 1944.

————, ed. *A Treasury of New England Folklore*. New York: Crown Publishers, 1965.

————, ed. *A Treasury of Southern Folklore*. New York: Crown Publishers, 1949.

Briggs, Katherine M. *A Dictionary of British Folk-Tales*. 4 vols. Bloomington, Ind.: Indiana University Press, 1967.

Brunvand, Jan H. *The Study of American Folklore*. 2nd ed. New York: W. W. Norton & Co., 1978.

————. *Urban American Legends*. New York: W. W. Norton & Co., 1980.

Burrison, John A. *"The Golden Arm": The Folk Tale and Its Literary Use by Mark Twain and Joel C. Harris*. Atlanta: Georgia State College School of Arts and Sciences Research Paper, 1968.

*Cerf, Bennett. *Famous Ghost Stories*. New York: Random House, 1944.

Chambers, Robert. *Popular Rhymes of Scotland*. London, Edinburgh: W. & R. Chambers, 1870. Reprint edition, Detroit: Singing Tree Press, 1969.

Chase, Richard, ed. *American Folk Tales and Songs*. New York: New American Library of World Literature, 1956. Reprint edition, New York: Dover Publications, 1971.

*————, ed. *Grandfather Tales*. Boston: Houghton Mifflin Co., 1948.

Cox, John H. *Folk-Songs of the South*. Cambridge, Mass.: Harvard University Press, 1925.

Creighton, Helen. *Bluenose Ghosts*. Toronto: Ryerson Press, 1957.

Dégh, Linda. "The 'Belief Legend' in Modern Society: Form, Function, and Relationship to Other Genres." In Wayland D. Hand, ed., *American Folk Legend, A Symposium*. Berkeley, Cal.: University of California Press, 1971.

Dorson, Richard M. *American Folklore*. Chicago: University of Chicago Press, 1959.

Flanders, Helen H., and George Brown. *Vermont Folk-Songs & Ballads*. Brattleboro, Vt.: Stephen Daye Press, 1932.

Fowke, Edith. *Folklore of Canada*. Toronto: McClelland and Stewart, 1976.

Gainer, Robert W. *Folklore of the Southern Appalachians*. Grantsville, W. Va.: Seneca Books, 1975.

Gardner, Emelyn E. *Folklore from the Schoharie Hills, New York*. Ann Arbor, Mich.: University of Michigan Press, 1937.

Halliwell-Phillips, James O. *The Nursery Rhymes of England*. London: Warne & Company, 1842.

Harris, Joel Chandler. *Nights With Uncle Remus: Myths and Legends of the Old Plantation*. Boston: Houghton Mifflin Co., 1882.

Hole, Christina. *Haunted England: A Survey of English Ghost-Lore*. London: B. T. Batsford, 1950.

*James, M. R. *The Collected Ghost Stories of M. R. James*. London: Edward Arnold & Co., 1931.

Johnson, Clifton. *What They Say in New England and Other American Folklore*. Boston: Lee and Shepherd, 1896. Reprint edition, Carl A. Withers, ed. New York: Columbia University Press, 1963.

Jones, Louis C. *Things That Go Bump in the Night*. New York: Hill and Wang, 1959.

Knapp, Mary and Herbert. *One Potato, Two Potato: The Secret Education of American Children*. New York: W. W. Norton & Co., 1976.

*Leach, Maria. *Rainbow Book of American Folk Tales and Legends*. Cleveland and New York: World Publishing Co., 1958.

———, ed. "Revenant." *Standard Dictionary of*

Folklore, Mythology and Legend. New York: Funk & Wagnalls Publishing Co., 1972.

*————. *The Thing at the Foot of the Bed and Other Scary Stories.* Cleveland and New York: World Publishing Co., 1959.

*————. *Whistle in the Graveyard.* New York: The Viking Press, 1974.

Montell, William M. *Ghosts Along the Cumberland: Deathlore in the Kentucky Foothills.* Knoxville, Tenn.: University of Tennessee Press, 1975.

Musick, Ruth Ann. *The Telltale Lilac Bush and Other West Virginia Ghost Tales.* Lexington, Ky.: University of Kentucky Press, 1965.

Opie, Iona and Peter. *The Lore and Language of Schoolchildren.* London: Oxford University Press, 1959.

————. *The Oxford Dictionary of Nursery Rhymes.* Oxford, England: Clarendon Press, 1951.

Puckett, Newbell N. *Folk Beliefs of the Southern Negro.* Chapel Hill, N.C.: University of North Carolina Press, 1926.

Randolph, Vance. *Ozark Folksongs.* Columbia, Mo.: State Historical Society of Missouri, 1949.

————. *Ozark Superstitions.* New York: Columbia University Press, 1947. Reprint edition, *Ozark Magic and Folklore.* New York: Dover Publications, 1964.

————. *Sticks in the Knapsack and Other Ozark Folk Tales.* New York: Columbia University Press, 1958.

————. *The Talking Turtle and Other Ozark Folk Tales.* New York: Columbia University Press, 1957.

Roberts, Leonard. *Old Greasybeard: Tales from the Cumberland Gap.* Detroit: Folklore Associates, 1969. Reprint edition, Pikeville, Ky.: Pikeville College Press, 1980.

————. *South from Hell-fer-Sartin: Kentucky Mountain*

Folk Tales. Lexington, Ky.: University of Kentucky Press, 1955. Reprint edition, Pikeville, Ky.: Pikeville College Press, 1964.

————. *Up Cutshin and Down Greasy: The Couches' Tales and Songs.* Lexington, Ky.: University of Kentucky Press, 1959. Reprinted as *Sang Branch Settlers: Folksongs and Tales of an Eastern Kentucky Family*, Pikeville, Ky.: Pikeville College Press, 1980.

Sandburg, Carl. *The American Songbag.* New York: Harcourt, Brace & Co., 1927.

Shakespeare, William. *The Works of William Shakespeare.* New York: Oxford University Press, 1938.

White, Newman I. *American Negro Folk-Songs.* Cambridge, Mass.: Harvard University Press, 1928.

Articles

Bacon, A. M., and Parsons, E. C. "Folk-Lore from Elizabeth Cith County, Va." *JAF* 35 (1922):250–327.

Barnes, Daniel R. "Some Functional Horror Stories on the Kansas University Campus." *SFQ* 30 (1966):305–12.

Beardsley, Richard K., and Hankey, Rosalie. "The Vanishing Hitchhiker." *CFQ* 1 (1942):303–36.

————. "The History of the Vanishing Hitchhiker." *CFQ* 2 (1943):3–25.

Boggs, Ralph Steele. "North Carolina White Folktales and Riddles." *JAF* 47 (1934):289–328.

Brown, Jennifer. "The Cure and Feeding of Windigo: A Critique." *American Anthropologist* 73 (1971):20–21.

Cord, Xenia E. "Further Notes on 'The Assailant in the Back Seat.'" *IF* 2 (1969):50–54.

Cox, John H. "Negro Tales from West Virginia." *JAF* 47 (1934):341–57.

Crowe, Hume. "The Wendigo and the Bear Who

Walks." *NMFR* 11 (1963–64):22–23.

Dégh, Linda. "The Hook and the Boy Friend's Death," *IF* 1 (1968):92–106.

Dorson, Richard. "The Folklore of Colleges." *The American Mercury* 68 (1949):671–77.

———. "The Runaway Grandmother." *IF* 1 (1968):68–69.

———. "The Roommate's Death and Related Dormitory Stories in Formation." *IF* 2 (1969):55–74.

Doyle, Charles Clay. "'As the Hearse Goes By': The Modern Child's *Memento Mori*." PTFS 40 (1976):175–90.

Drake, Carlos. "The Killer in the Back Seat." *IF* 1 (1968):107–109.

Fauset, Arthur Huff. "Tales and Riddles Collected in Philadelphia." *JAF* 41 (1928):529–57.

Halpert, Herbert. "The Rash Dog and the Bloody Head." *HFB* 1 (1942):9–11.

Himelick, Raymond. "Classical Versions of 'The Poisoned Garment.'" *HF* 5 (1946):83–84.

Ives, Edward D. "The Haunted House and the Headless Ghost." *NEF* 4 (1962):61–67.

Jones, Louis C. "Hitchhiking Ghosts of New York." *CFQ* 4 (1945):284–92.

Kennedy, Ruth. "The Silver Toe." PTFS 6 (1927):41–42.

Nuttall, Zelia. "A Note on Ancient Mexican Folk-Lore." *JAF* 8 (1895):117–29.

Parochetti, JoAnn Stephens. "Scary Stories from Purdue." *KFQ* 10 (1965):49–57.

Parsons, Elsie Crews. "Tales from Guilford County, North Carolina." *JAF* 30 (1917):168–208.

Randolph, Vance. "Folk Tales from Arkansas." *JAF* 65 (1952):159–66.

Reaver, J. Russell. "'Embalmed Alive': A Developing Urban Ghost Tale." *NYFQ* 8 (1952):217–20.

Speck, Frank G. "Penobscot Tales and Religious Beliefs." *JAF* 48 (1935):1–107.

Stewart, Susan. "The Epistemology of the Scary Story." Scholarly article in process, 1980.

Stimson, Anna K. "Cries of Defiance and Derision, and Rhythmic Chants of West Side New York City (1893–1903)." *JAF* 58 (1945):124–29.

Theroux, Paul. "Christmas Ghosts." *The New York Times Book Review* (Dec. 23, 1979):1, 15.

Thigpen, Kenneth A., Jr. "Adolescent Legends in Brown County: A Survey." *IF* 4 (1971):183–207.

Vlach, John M. "One Black Eye and Other Horrors: A Case for the Humorous Anti-Legend." *IF* 4 (1971):95–124.

ACKNOWLEDGMENTS

The following persons helped me to prepare this book:

Kendall Brewer, Frederick Seibert Brewer III, and Shawn Barry, who sat in the loft of a barn with me in Maine and told me scary stories.

The Boy Scouts at Camp Roosevelt at East Eddington, Maine, who told me their scary stories.

Several folklorists who shared with me their knowledge and scholarly resources, particularly Kenneth Goldstein of the University of Pennsylvania, Edward D. Ives of the University of Maine, and Susan Stewart of Temple University.

Other scholars whose articles and collections were important sources of information.

Librarians at the University of Maine (Orono), the University of Pennsylvania, Princeton University, and at the folklore archives listed on page 89.

My wife, Barbara, who did the musical notation in Chapters 1 and 3, carried out bibliographical research, and contributed in other ways.

I thank each of them.

—A. S.